T0354999

LOVELESSLY

LOVELESSLY

ROBERT T. FLOYD JR.

Archway Publishing books may be ordered through booksellers or by contacting:

Archway Publishing
1663 Liberty Drive
Bloomington, IN 47403
www.archwaypublishing.com
844-669-3957

ISBN: 978-1-6657-7339-3 (sc)
ISBN: 978-1-6657-7340-9 (e)

Library of Congress Control Number: 2025903081

Print information available on the last page.

Archway Publishing rev. date: 03/25/2025

"Every work of fiction is a peep-show, in which we observe the spasms and convulsions of the agonized human heart."

SCHOPENHAUER

CHAPTER 1

ANDREW WELLS

AT THE TURN OF THE 19TH CENTURY, THE TOWN FOLK OF SOUTH Kensington lived modest lives while raising their children. Much of the children's training is centered on the church. God had favored the British before all other nations and provided them with knowledge, understanding, and firmness of character. As a result, the British are degraded and sometimes held in contempt. The teachings of religion had instilled in their minds a sense of fairness and justice. Andrew Wells completed his studies, and like most of London's young lads wondered what he should do with the remainder of his life. He had grown tired of sitting-in on lectures at Cambridge. Andrew did not wish to become a career student, part of the grading system. He listened and formed his own ideas. Andrew decided to serve the crown by becoming a soldier. Under the law, impressment meant he must follow the urgings of the British government. Britain sought to regain control of her former colony in America following defeat in the war of 1776. Tensions between the two nations had flared as a consequence of British support for the Indian tribes who were being pushed off of huge portions of land these tribes had lived on for centuries. During his training, Andrew is questioned by high ranking officials of the British military regarding his participation in classes at Cambridge, without being registered as a student. It seemed a special branch of the military maintained confidential relationships with teachers and administrators. Once Andrew arrived in America, along with the columns of British troops, the atrocities of war soon revealed themselves. Many of his fellow soldiers died as a result of disease or infection from untreated injury. Open wounds were infested with flies who laid their eggs, which in a matter of hours resulted in maggots.

Following their assault on Detroit on August 16, 1812 the American general surrendered along with his army to British troops. Andrew Wells had hardly fired his musket during the battle. The British Royal navy set-up a blockade of the Atlantic coast, alerting Andrew to a problem that would continue to haunt him for years to come. It was the problem of negro slavery that existed in the United States. During the blockade, 4,000 slaves escaped onto British ships where they were welcomed and freed. Many took part in the Battle of Bladensburg and the burning of Washington, D.C. The bloody war was about the acquisition of territory occupied by red men, in order that black men kidnapped from the shores of west Africa could cultivate that land as slaves. Land expansion everywhere and slavery is the path to fabulous wealth. Greediness for more territory and greater increase of slavery is widely sought. Fifteen-thousand Americans perished during the war, and more than nine-thousand British and Canadian soldiers met their deaths. The thousands of native Americans and Africans who died were mere victims of collateral damage. In a conflict like this, there are no winners or losers, it merely illustrates man's inhumanity to man. The United States Congress signed a treaty almost three years into the fighting ending the war of 1812.

Andrew Wells decided to remain in the United States, settling in south Texas near Beaumont. Life in London and his frivolous existence in Kensington seemed years and centuries ago. Expansion of slave territory had brought war in Texas against Mexico. Justice McLean of the United States Supreme Court believed that further expansion might lead to the overthrow of the government. "Without the sanction of law, slavery can no more exist in a territory than a man can breathe without air," the Justice remarked. Andrew took note that many of his Texas neighbors wanted to expand their laws into New Mexico, Nevada, Utah, and Wyoming. Andrew Wells carved-out his own small area to build a home and till the soil. He had no desire to become a slave owner. "Just as I would not be a slave, I have no desire to own other human beings," Andrew said. A major issue manifested as a consequence of the many slaves who escaped their owner's plantations to states in the north. The fugitive slave, once captured, was taken before a judge who would issue a certificate authorizing slave-catchers the right of removal of the fugitive to the state from which he had fled.

In an October 1820 case in Philadelphia, counsel for the fugitive spoke of a meeting at which resolutions were adopted advising blacks to arm themselves against law-enforcement and shoot down officers of the law. If such advise were taken, the killing of the first officer would be a signal for extermination of the black race. The judge in the case replied: "God knows that I detest slavery, but it is an existing evil and we must endure it, and give it such protection, till we can get rid of it without destroying the last hope of free government."

In 1825 a slave woman who had escaped from her owner in Cecil county, Maryland, fled to Delaware, where she married and moved to New Jersey. There a son was born in 1829. The couple visited Philadelphia to buy and trade at the markets. The Maryland slave owner advised slave-catchers who captured slaves for ransom asking that she be brought back to Maryland. Following the kidnapping and return of the woman, Pennsylvania authorities charged the slave-catchers with the crime. An appeal to the governor by Pennsylvania's governor went unanswered. War between the states seemed inevitable as slave-catchers crossed state lines with impunity. Slave hunters from Maryland continued to enter Pennsylvania citing the Fugitive slave act. Blacks who had armed themselves while preparing for the slave hunters suffered injury and death in battle. There were many incidents of violence between slave hunters and blacks in Pennsylvania along the Maryland border including federal officers of the Marshal service. The judges, law-enforcement officers, slave owners, slave-catchers, and blacks themselves were all in conflict. In the eye of an outsider like Andrew Wells, the situation represented total chaos.

My neighbors and friends in Texas have no idea that I'm a former British soldier who came to this country to fight a war. I'm just an observer. What I've seen is the mad rush for wealth through the labor of chattel slavery. Recently I learned of a negro from Kentucky who had apparently escaped into Ohio where he lived as a free person for a number of years. Set upon by slave catchers, the negro was taken into court to be ordered returned to his master. In court rooms from Boston to Philadelphia the question of whether escaped negros should be returned to masters in Georgia and Alabama continued to find their way before the bench. In Boston, a judge found the Fugitive Slave Act unconstitutional. Justice Curtis of the United States Supreme Court, a supporter of the act decided to leave the court and return to private practice.

Anthony Burns, a negro, was brought before a U.S. Commissioner in Boston with the demand that he be removed as the property of a Virginia claimant. A mob stormed the court house, carried the fugitive away, and killed one of the deputy marshals. One section of the country found odious the notion of fugitive human stock from labor, while another section insists on the enforcement of the law. A judge in Illinois, arguing with regard to the importation of slaves said "Negros have been and continue to be a vagabond population, and to prevent their influx into the state, laws have been passed," There are 350,000 slave owners in a population of 23,000,000 in the 1820's. Chief Justice Taney of the United States Supreme Court issued a vote of confidence to assure southerners that the court would uphold the institution of slavery. One state would not respect the laws of another.

This country continued to astound me as such a strange place. They claim all men are created equal, yet that does not include black men who are slaves, and red men who are forced into the extreme north-west, New Mexico, and Arizona. Their supreme law, the constitution, declares at Article one, section two: "Any person who was not free would be counted as three-fifths of a free individual…" Not yet a whole person. How a society can expect to survive with this kind of division is a mystery. I had become aware of the humanity of these individuals held in bondage. They were in-fact, no different than I in terms of their desire to be free. The proof rests in how many had escaped to states that outlawed slavery and the ongoing disputes in the courts. The white women live in a vacuum, not slaves, yet not free, indifferent, they exist. A slave woman in Texas, fogged with a rawhide whip bled profusely from the beating of lashes well laid-on. When the poor woman was untied, her back was covered in blood. She was whipped terribly, but she continued to denounce the overseer and shouted every vile epithet of which she could think. Her blood mixed with her milk when breast-feeding her baby. Because she seized every opportunity to break free from the plantation, she was eventually held prisoner in an iron collar. A fugitive slave woman trapped by slave-catchers in Ohio killed her own daughter and tried to kill herself. She rejoiced that her child was dead. "Now she will never know what a woman suffers as a slave." The woman pleaded to be placed on-trial for murder. "I will go singing to the gallows rather than be returned to slavery," she said. Then came the case that would close the door on all others.

A slave by the name of Dred Scott resided in Illinois after being transported there by his master in 1818. Illinois prohibited slavery. After residing there for a number of years with his wife and two children, Scott went into court asking to become a free person. The judge granted Scott's request in accord with the state's constitution. However, when Scott crossed into Missouri, his right to be free was gone, and his wife and children became nothing but mere pieces of property. Dred Scott appealed to the United States Supreme Court. The court granted the appeal stating the case would be heard at the next term beginning in December. Dred Scott issued a public plea: "I am now in the hands of the sheriff of this country. I have no money to pay anybody at Washington to speak for me. My fellow men, can any of you help me in my day of trial." President James Buchanan stated emphatically that the question of slavery "agitation" needed to be settled once and for all. When a political scheme is to be furthered by judicial action, it is a thousand times better than that action taken by congress. The Supreme Court's decision, written by Chief Justice Roger B. Taney held: "The negro was not included, and not intended to be included under the word citizen in the constitution, and therefore could claim none of the rights and privileges secured to the citizens of the United States. The history of our country, as well as, the language of Declaration of Independence and the Constitution point to the fact, that the negro has no rights that the white man is bound to respect." Dred Scott and his family were to remain slaves until death. Justice Curtis submitted his resignation from the court, following argument with the chief justice, and so the Dred Scott case further deepened the racial divide. It seemed inevitable that conflict was at hand over a document at war with itself. As a British subject, I did not wish to return to London, yet I needed to relieve myself of a racial powder-keg. I am walking on barrels of powder. With few exceptions, the minds of Americans appear to be incapable of addressing any question which involves ordinary fairness for slaves. Chief Justice Taney subsequently acknowledged that negros were for the most part credulous, and easily mislead by stronger minds. He was not a slaveholder, that all of his slaves he emancipated more than thirty years ago, except two, who were too old to provide for themselves. Dred Scott died within one year, and his wife soon afterward, while the storm over the case continued.

The decision in Scott vs Sanford sounded the death-knell to abolitionists. The battle to save slavery and the beginning of the second American revolution was underway. Texas was among the several states that seceded from the union of the United States. For the first time in history, an oligarchy of slave owners created a flag over the symbol of slavery. I had come to this country as a soldier for the crown of England. I leave exhausted by ongoing war and struggle. I have completed the mission. The brig I boarded at the port of New Orleans set-sail to the west Indies.

CHAPTER 2

SAN DOMINGO

LOVELESSLY MOREAU LIVES IN A WORLD OF MIRRORS, WHERE THE reflections of life flash in all directions. Her father, Francois is French, her mother Carlee, African. A moment of lust shared between plantation owner and his slave had produced a child of mixed race. Lovelessly enjoys the privilege of being considered a free person, yet she is not allowed to sit at the dinner table when guests arrive. Basic household chores are reserved for the servants, including Carlee. Therefore Lovelessly suffers from the blight of slavery and the lack of education. She passes her days amid singing slave girls, few friends, or social life. Strongly brewed rum is cheap, the fame of the mulatto girls of La Cap is widely known, while countryside life is mental isolation, large plantation houses with sparse furnishings, devoid of taste. San Domingo is a place between heaven and hell. Francois came to the island seeking fortune. His plantation covers a vast area managing the labor of four-hundred slaves. It is beneath the dignity of a rich man to have less than four times as many slaves as he needs.

Francois Moreau's wife Camille arrived in San Domingo with her husband. She accepts Lovelessly as her own child. Camille had encouraged her husband to lay with the slave woman to bear him a child since she was beyond the years for the fruit of the womb, and she wished to fulfill her husband's desire for offspring. The scarcity of white women made relations between colonists and their black female slaves inevitable. Consequently their offspring can never enter the white class. For once considered white, they could lay claim to public office and honor. This was the hard truth, yet wise and necessary in a land of fifteen slaves to one white. Once the law of reversion takes hold, nature's principle assumes its power and mulattos tend to lean toward the negro.

European nations found themselves in conflict with one another over the island, its population, and resources. In the past few years, French peasants had stormed the Bastille with cries of liberty and equality. These cries were heard in San Domingo where 28,000 whites owned 405,000 negro slaves. There are also 22,000 free colored persons. At the turn of the century, revolution in the motherland had spread to the island colony. The great planters or oligarchs held inferior whites in contempt, who in-turn despise people of color and free blacks, who in-turn look down upon slaves. Such are the foundations of the colonial system, that rests upon slavery and the prejudice of color. Only the smallest spark could ignite the highly inflammable material resting in the bosom of Francois Moreau.

Carlee loved to sit and talk with Lovelessly. Carlee informed the young girl of the perils she and thousands of other slaves experienced at Elmina castle on the coast of west Africa. The castle was a fortress, bound by cannons at ready fire. The captors utilized torture and beatings to maintain compliance. She explained the ruthless breeding tactics used against female slaves. Those who failed to conform were thrown into an open shaft in the ground of the dungeon which lead into the sea and drowning. A dungeon marked by a human skull and crossed bones housed the corpses of slaves tortured to death. A Biblical inscription over the dungeon read: "Servant be obedient to your master." The dungeon of no return was the final exit onto awaiting ships that set-sail with their human cargo. Carlee explained that many slaves leap into the sea, choosing death rather than bondage. For every five-hundred that were taken away from the Gold Coast, only one-hundred arrived at San Domingo. "Once we arrived, we had nothing to look forward to morning after morning, but the sizzling heat, rawhide whip of the overseer, long rows of cotton."

Francois hired a tutor who instructed Lovelessly in French, English, the piano, and the arts. The white children were sent on the six week voyage to the motherland for schooling and a break from the heat. The European must always be on guard, the sun is a danger. Good health is maintained by abstemious living. For whites, creole or European, rich or poor, criminal or governor, they are all white and determined to rule San Domingo.

"They are my friends, once the heart is engaged, then you suddenly realize that we are all just human," Lovelessly explains.

"The great misfortune is to marry into a family that will carry you only as their shame," Carlee replies.

San Domingo had obtained a height of prosperity unsurpassed in the history of European colonies. The greatest part of the soil is covered by plantations on a gigantic scale which supplies half of Europe with sugar, coffee, and cotton. The degree of prosperity increased by leaps and bounds. Sugar and coffee plantations covered every mountainside from Port au Prince in the west to Sabana in the east .La Cap is far superior in appearance to Port au Prince which has the appearance of a low-class area. Seventy-five percent of the white population is European born. It will take two generations before the race can strike foot in the island. This is a population of fortune hunters, not settlers, and the return to France is ever in mind. Slavery had become the very basis of society.

Lovelessly grows-up a recluse, yet not by choice. The neighbors hardly know one another. Francois would return to Paris, flouting his wealth from exile by the jewelry and clothing he wears, yet merchants laugh behind his back and strip his money while prostitutes join in the take. The slave revolt, fruit of the poisonous tree, grows out of the assault on the Bastille. It is marked by vicious, cruel, inhuman, and satanic-like treatment. Slaves called Maroons had taken to San Domingo's tropical forests. They had grown tired of poisoning and stealing the herds of their owners. Seated around the huge mahogany table, while servants prepare their meals, Francois, Camille, and several slave owners discuss the situation in San Domingo.

"The colonies cannot exist without slavery," Francois begins.

"The loyalty of the mulattos is doubtful, while the blacks are ripe for revolt and massacre," an owner replies.

Lovelessly is seated on the foyer, yet her ear listens intently. Francois summons his daughter to join the discussion. "What do you think Lovelessly, regarding the revolt of the slaves?" Francois asks

"I do not fully understand father…things have always been peaceful."

"We must maintain the infamous traffic on the coast of Africa. The government must do that, or renounce the colonies, 30,000 whites cannot control 406,000 savages only by force of opinion, vituperative language, which tends to destroy that opinion," a slave owner replies.

"The revolution is almost entirely the work of a single man, Toussaint Louverture," Francois explains.

"Louverture has lectured his legions on the virtues of Milton's Paradise Lost, as they regard the revolution in the motherland," an oligarch replies.

The horrors and cruelties that followed make nature shudder. To arrest and hang became synonymous. To drown two-hundred individuals is a step towards national unity. To be torn in pieces by blood-hounds or buried alive is to cleanse. Every negro or mulatto who had been a free person is ordered returned to slavery. The French troops are sickened by disease. Of 60,000 troops sent from France, little more than 4,000 survive. The blood continued to flow like the waves off the Atlantic. The odor in the air is tainted with pestilence. In the first two months of the revolt, 2,000 whites are massacred. More than one-hundred sugar, coffee, and cotton plantations had been destroyed. The buildings on these plantations had been consumed by fire. Twelve-hundred families are reduced to abject destitution, 10,000 slaves had been massacred. The black stockades were demolished, the skulls of prisoners killed by un-speakable tortures roll on the earth. The main road leading to the camps are strung with the hanged bodies of rebels.

Once additional French troops arrive at Port au Prince they proclaim that the National Assembly has decreed blacks and mulattos as free persons, equal to whites. Yet the French general faced a dilemma. The crimes that have been committed are so atrocious that it is impossible to pardon them. It is perfectly clear, that mulattos are as much opposed as whites to negro emancipation. Consequently, if the whites would fully accept mulattos as their equals, it is certain they could join wholeheartedly in the suppression of the rebel slaves. Francois and a few other plantation owners gather to discuss the developing situation.

"There can be no agriculture without slavery. That five-hundred thousand savages cannot be brought from the shores of Africa to be free French citizens here is incompatible with our European brethren," Francois begins.

"But we must dispatch a fleet of brigs to replace depleted stocks that have perished during the uprising," comes the reply.

"The pirates wish us to pay insurance and other imagined loss."

"The government makes a huge mistake, if it thinks that any of us will ever live in friendly familiarity with the negro or the negress. The law cannot command the feelings of the heart."

"San Domingo is an island where Frenchmen rule over numerous plantations, which cover the entire surface. How can sixty-thousand of us expect four-hundred thousand savages to bow before us? If we want peace, half the white population must depart for the motherland."

"In Le Cap the burning homes of whites continues under the torments of black soldiers."

"Members of different African tribes must be carefully split-up to lessen conspiracy, and they are compelled to master our language, highly complex products of centuries of civilization," Francois explains.

While racial groups fight, England and Spain send troops to obtain San Domingo for themselves. The fighting illustrates a horror unsurpassed. The only prisoners taken, are those reserved for torture. So ferocious is the race hatred of the combatants that men tear one another to pieces with their teeth. Louverture's forces eventually crush the mulatto army. Many mulattos set-sail for St. Thomas, while others flee to Cuba. Toussaint Louverture makes a triumphant entry into Les Cayes.

General Louverture defeated General Rigiald and claimed the title of Emperor for life with power to name a successor. A virtual declaration of independence from France. Black men who had formerly been slaves fill high positions in the government. In an effort to sustain the economy, Louverture negotiates trade agreements with the United Kingdom and the United States. He maintained his large and well trained army. The "Code Noir" which mandated that slaves be made Catholics, stripped of their African names is blasted asunder.

The self-proclaimed Emperor addressed those assembled to hear him speak to the nation. "I swear to maintain the integrity of the territory, and independence of the kingdom; never to suffer, under any pretext whatsoever, the revival of slavery, or any feudal measure inconsistent with liberty and the exercise of the civil and political rights of the people of Haiti, the original name of our country which had been forbidden under the colonial system of the French."

Lovelessly astounded the gathering inside the concert hall with her playing of the piano, in honor of the nation's new governor Toussaint Louverture. Peace may have finally come to the troubled island. Seated in the audience, Andrew Wells acknowledges with warm applause. The ship Andrew boarded at New Orleans had docked at port Santo Domingo for water, rations, and other supplies before sailing for the United Kingdom. Receiving praise from her parents, Francois and Camille, following the performance, Andrew Wells steps forward introducing himself.

"You are English, are you a soldier?" Francois asks.

"I was a soldier…I went to war in the United States. I'm returning to the United Kingdom," Andrew replies.

"You have a lovely daughter, I enjoyed her music very much," Andrew continues.

"Yes she was raised correctly," Francois says.

"Can we have something to drink on the foyer?" Andrew asks turning to Lovelessly.

"Yes of course," she replies.

Seated at a table overlooking the beach and the powerful waves coming ashore, Andrew Wells continues.

"You are of mixed race."

"Yes my mother is a domestic servant on my father's plantation."

"Is he a slave owner?"

"Yes, there are four-hundred slaves on the plantation."

"Slavery is a huge problem…I was sent to America to fight a war because red men were being forced to leave their land in order that black men kidnapped from Africa could toil that land as slaves."

"Some of our people fled to the United States rather than accept the new governor. Are there many slaves in America?

"There are four-million, they have been there for more than two-hundred years. I wanted to stay there, but it is a society at war with itself."

"What exactly does that mean?" Lovelessly asks.

"Here is a country that says all men are created equal, yet that does not apply to red men or black men. Those of lighter shades, soft hair texture, and rainbow eyes are high yellows or redbone, yet they are still considered negros. Their slave owning fathers live in respectable denial. All slave children are by law the chattel of the father. President Thomas Jefferson owned six-hundred slaves. He fathered six children with his slave mistress Sally Hemings," Andrew explains.

"You must forgive me Andrew, I am so naïve I thought San Domingo was the only place like that. I was born here in this world of mirrors, that reflect only the contradictions of this island," Lovelessly explains.

"Whites in the United States maintain numerical supremacy, it's just the opposite here. Why are you called Lovelessly? I could very easily love you. When I peer into those beautiful turquoise eyes, I see nothing but love."

"That is very sweet of you. My father says I was raised correctly, that means Lovelessly. You have been around the world, there is much to be learned from someone like you."

"While we were at sea, the news came that President Abraham Lincoln had been shot and killed. This was the greatest American president. He had signed a document emancipating the slaves. A manhunt through Maryland and Virginia pursued the assassin before killing him. Four others involved in the conspiracy to kill Lincoln were hung by the neck until they were dead, including a woman," Andrew explains.

"Slavery brings so much misery and grief where it exists," Lovelessly replies.

"That's true, great civilizations like Greece, Egypt, and Rome have fallen into the junk-heap of history because they were built on the backs of slaves. Lincoln did not believe whites and blacks could live together, and he expressed those feelings to black leaders. He feared the north would be overrun by four-million ex-slaves, therefore he signed an agreement to use federal funds to relocate 5,000 former slaves from the United States to Lle a Vache island, a small twenty square mile island off the southwest coast of San Domingo.

Federal compensation was also ordered to be paid slaveowners who lost their human property due to emancipation."

"I never heard that story, Lli a Vache is just south of Port au Prince."

"It turned out to be a disaster, many died from smallpox, the homes, schools, and hospitals they were promised never materialized. People slept on the ground and lived off the soil."

"What a shame, it's just like our nightmare in San Domingo."

"Lincoln exchanged letters with Karl Marx. Marx wrote his Das Kapital at 28 Dean street in my home town, London. An oligarchy of slaveowners frowned on the exchange of ideas between Marx and Lincoln. They created the conspiracy to kill the president."

"All of this is a bit much for me," Lovelessly says.

"In time, I will teach you."

"But you are leaving San Domingo, I will never see you again."

They stroll along the beach after their drinks. "I will return, I can never forget you Lovelessly." Their first kiss is a thrilling event, reaching the depths of their very being.

"Where did you obtain the wisdom and knowledge you possess?" Lovelessly asks.

"Once I completed regular school, I was intrigued by Cambridge, the second oldest university in my country. I wondered what went on there. My father talked about that school, he worked for the government, yet he wished to keep my mother uninformed about his work. I would walk into the lecture halls, and listen to the teachers. There is much to be learned by listening."

"So you did not receive a grade or certificate?"

"To be a wise individual, it is necessary to utilize information to one's own benefit and to survive in this strange and dangerous world."

"I have never met anyone like you Andrew, when you leave, I'll never see you again."

"We will be together Lovelessly, I promise you... If you will wait for me, we will be together."

CHAPTER THREE

EXODUS

THE FRENCH MINISTER IN SAN DOMINGO CONTACTED NAPOLEON Bonaparte urging him to send more troops to restore French rule, and to crush the Louverture regime. War with England had taken priority in the homeland. The British have the problem of generating enough tax revenue to finance the war. A London group set-up a private bank which loaned 1.2 million pounds to the crown at 8% interest. This set-up of the Bank of England was beneficial, a permanent loan that the king promised to pay by taxing enough to pay the interest. A permanent loan meant the principal is never to be repaid and the bank made a profit from the sum of annual interest paid on the loan. The English empire extended to five continents, while France held large sectors of Africa. "The men whom you send thither must act with tact, prudence, and dissimulation towards the negro," the minister said. He further advised that white women who have prostituted themselves to negros, whatever their rank, should be sent to France to be executed.

The arrival of the French troops begins military tactics and troop movements across the island, leaving thousands dead and towns scorched to the earth. Toussaint Louverture is lured to a secure location by the French General Brunet who offers peace talks. Once Louverture arrives, the general states "His excellency will extend the rights of French subjects and citizens, which are undoubtedly better than to be treated as barbarians, savages, or maroon negros." Louverture rejects the offer as no offer at all, therefore he is set-upon, his entourage massacred." Is this how you observe the faith of your treaties?"he asks. Louverture is arrested, gagged, and shackled, like a felon while at the table of General Brunet. Subsequently he is deported to France and held at Fort de-Joux. amid the horrors of a dungeon, cold and torture. A trial ends in judgment ordering Louverture be hung by the neck until dead inside the football stadium at high noon. The slave trade is restored in San Domingo and it is decreed that new arrivals from Africa are mere chattel. Those on the island who had enjoyed freedom, are re-enslaved. Mulattos are also deprived of equal rights. The color line is firmly restored and mixed marriages prohibited. A new insurrection is planned and set into motion. The French Minister again contacts Bonaparte: "To have been rid of Toussaint Louverture is not enough, there are two-thousand more leaders to get rid of as well." The Minister further complains that negro soldiers recruited for the cause of France are totally untrustworthy. "Recently a whole battalion killed its white officers and deserted, for the struggle is strictly race war."

With the Minister's message in-hand, Napoleon Bonaparte must consider the extermination of the island's black population. "So long as there remains at San Domingo any considerable body of negros who for twelve years have made war, the colony will never be re-established. All negros and negress slaves, the latter being more cruel than the men, must be done away with. These are frightful measures, but we must take them or renounce the colony." A black man called Macandel from Senegal possessing a religious philosophy announced himself as the "Black Messiah," come to cleanse the island of all whites. The negros consider him a God. Macandel's plan is vested on the wholesale use of poison. The master, his children, his cattle and slaves are the target. In Le Cap, the water is poisoned to exterminate the colonists. An informer reveals the conspiracy, and Macandel is hunted-down and hanged.

While Lovelessly Moreau finds her way through the brush leading to the mansion, she observes several rebel insurgents converging on the property with weapons in-hand. Lovelessly takes cover immediately shielding herself. Suddenly screams are heard from within the house, followed by gunshots. A moment of silence is followed by more loud voices and more gunshots. The rebels then rush out of the house, leaving it partially aflame. Lovelessly hurriedly enters the front door, observing the carnage of a slaughter. Her mother Carlee, and Camille both lie shot dead. All of the other house servants lie dead throughout the house. Lovelessly must get out since the fire spreads rapidly. A door slams shut in an adjacent corridor. Lovelessly fears some of the killers may still be inside the house. Fear is turned to joy upon observing Francois emerge. She rushes into his arms, while he surveys the scene.

"I went into the underground passage when I heard the first shots, I didn't have time to alert anyone," Francois explains.

"We must go to La Cap to find refuse," Lovelessly replies.

The English population on the island board ships bound for the United States and the U.K. Francois and Lovelessly set-sail for France. A proclamation is promulgated by rebel leaders offering favorable conditions for all exiles to return to San Domingo. But no sooner than they returned, an order is issued to massacre the English population. The murder of the English began at Port au Prince in January, and by March they were all murdered in mass without exception. The beautiful city of Le Cap lay in ruin. French San Domingo had vanished and the black state of Haiti emerged.

On board the ship headed for France, Francois attempts to calm the fears of those who have managed to escape the terror.

"As far as the negro is concerned, his triumph in Haiti will plunge to the jungle level of the Congo," he explains.

Huddled among the hundreds who have managed to escape the terror, Lovelessly wonders what life will be like on the other side of the Atlantic.

During her nineteen years of life, this is her first trip away from the island. In the past few days, she had witnessed the unspeakable horrors of the murders of her mother and step-mother, to the vastness of the ocean's surface.

"Are you alright?" Francois asks.

"Yes I'm fine, just wondering what it will be like when we arrive."

"You will love Paris. We have a villa with a perfect view of the tower."

"Father why do I not have a sister or a brother?"

"The tragedy of miscegenation is that it begins with sexual exploitation and ends with deep feeling. In the first book of the Holy Bible, we see where Rachel, the wife of Jacob has no children. Jacob explains: God has withheld from you the fruit of the womb. Rachel replies by urging Jacob to lay with her maid Bilah who bears him a son. Rachel's maid Bilah conceived again, and bore a second son. Two other sons were conceived by Jacob through another maid, then came a fifth and sixth son, also a daughter. Then God in all of his glory allowed Rachel to conceive a son of her own and she named him Joseph. Joseph's brothers saw that their father loved him more than all his brothers so they hated him. Joseph possessed the extraordinary ability to intrepid dreams, therefore the brothers plotted against him: Come let us kill him and throw him into the pit, and we will tell father that a wild beast has devoured him. Then we will see what becomes of his dreams. However, the brothers thought about their evil plot against their own flesh and blood so they decided to sell Joseph into slavery in Egypt. Yet Joseph found favor in Egypt as a result of his talents, therefore Pharaoh placed Joseph into a position second only to Pharaoh himself. Following the death of their father, Joseph's brothers feared retribution from God for what they had done. However, Joseph explained that what had happened was God's divine means of getting him into Egypt, where the Jewish people were slaves for four-hundred years. Pharaoh observed the slaves multiply to the point that eventually their numbers would surpass that of the Egyptians. Therefore Pharaoh decreed: Come let us deal wisely with them, lest they multiply and in the event of war, they join those who hate us, and fight against us, and depart from the land. In San Domingo we did not take heed to this lesson of population control. The slaves outnumbered us by fifteen to one. The rising tide of color propagates our flight to the motherland," Francois explains.

"That is really some story father, I must read it, yet I am surprised that you know this and still had four-hundred slaves on the plantation," Lovelessly replies.

"The pursuit of money causes one to look beyond that which is good and what is evil. In England women are still used instead of horses for hauling canal boats," Francois continues.

"That's hard work!"

"The money for horses or machines is expensive, these women are surplus population. The English are heathens," Francois explains.

The French Parliament sent a request to Francois Moreau to speak before the National Assembly regarding the situation at San Domingo. Francois accepted, stating he was honored by the request. Lovelessly was also excited, following her first impressions of Paris, and the hope that one day she could return to the island. Taking in the view as they cross the river Seine in their horse-drawn carriage, they walk past the statue of Francois D' Aguesseau, the nation's former Chancellor whom Voltaire called the most learned magistrate the nation ever had. Taking her seat in the huge concave auditorium, Lovelessly's eyes are fixated as her father approaches the podium.

"It is indeed an esteemed privilege to address such a distinguished audience in the nation's National Assembly. San Domingo attained a height of prosperity unsurpassed in the history of European colonies. The entire island is covered with plantations, supplying Europe with sugar, coffee, and cotton. The problem exacerbated through the island's population. One-half of one percent are white. There are more than 400,000 negro slaves deported from the coasts of Africa. Slavery became the very basis of society. The colony, such as it is, cannot exist without slavery. Once the slaves latched onto the concept of liberty taking place in the homeland, whites in San Domingo were in trouble. The basic factor in human affairs is not politics but race. In San Domingo, caste the system of hierarchy, that helped determine standing and respect, assumptions of beauty toward white females, and even who received the benefit of doubt fell apart. Caste is invisible, unseen, yet it undergirds inequality, injustice, and disparity. The world-wide struggle between the races of mankind is the fundamental problem of this century. Population control must be our number one priority. The negro, freed from slavery spells regression and his victory in San Domingo will plunge to the jungle level of the Congo. There is no more certain breeder of trouble, than the expansive urge of a fast breeding people, and the strength that comes from poverty and hardship. Asia like Africa must be partitioned, each section at the disposal of European countries. Going forth from Europe's teeming shores, whites have planted their laws, customs, and battle flags at the uttermost ends of the earth. This war with England is nothing short of a headlong plunge into white race suicide between closely related white stocks. Fight we must, but let not that fight be an internecine war against our own bloods. To allow the tropic belt around the world to fall into Asia's hands is like white race suicide. Nothing is more unchanging than the racial divisions of mankind. One needs but to compare the populations of France, Germany, Russia, and Japan to realize the real enemy is the birth rate. When an enormous thrust of yellow population pressure bursts into a white land, it crushes the white men out first, the white laborer, the white merchant, the white aristocrat, until every vestige of whites has gone from the land forever. It is not a nation of free people, it becomes what the English call a plantation. We cannot make a homogeneous population of people who do not blend with our European brethren. Japan's population pressure is a problem. The country constantly seeks areas for population expansion, lands where they can breed by the tens of millions. This is the secret of her aggressive foreign policy. The English believe they will rule India for centuries, taxing all of the Indian people. As was the case in San Domingo, where there is no white policeman, no white postman, no white society, while the flood gates open to half-breeds and negros, against the oligarchy in further crossing the races and freeing slaves, while miscegenation creeps forward with every successive generation, it explodes in revolt. China is likely to be mobilized for political reasons like revolt against white dominion or for social reasons like over population. Only the Chinaman himself can do that by controlling his reckless procreation. Over population is of itself a sufficiently serious problem. San Domingo was materially prosperous, yet socially diseased. The French empire will not falter as a consequence of San Domingo, there are vast areas of Africa and Asia to be civilized. The empire will live-on forever."

Lovelessly is stunned by her father's remarks, yet she had gained a valuable insight as to how the rich and powerful view the world in which she lives.

CHAPTER 4

CITY OF LIGHT

THE BRIGHT RAYS OF THE SUN BEAMING THROUGH THE CURTAINS awakens Lovelessly Moreau to a new day. She rises, stretches her arms, and approaches the window peering out at the city of light. The Eiffel Tower stands high in all its gargantuan splendor. "It just stands there, watching over everything and everybody," she says. Lovelessly wonders what is happening in San Domingo, whether the change of the country's name has brought peace? Following the short time she has been in Paris, Lovelessly realizes her world of the past had been a prison. "You do not have to be a slave, to be in bondage," she says. There is more freedom on one block of Paris, then the entire island of San Domingo. Carlee had once told her daughter that black people were free in Paris. Free to live where you wanted, work where you were qualified, and love whom you pleased.

Growing-up on an island in the Caribbean had been an isolated existence. She is not white, not black, not a slave, existing in the insecure world Francois created. Her private isolation extended once she ventured out onto a plantation where the labor of four-hundred slaves created untold wealth for her family. The isolation had been so intense, it ultimately alienated one from another, whether slave or free. In Paris, there is an invisible safety in numbers since assimilation is not a requirement once she accepts French culture and way of life. Lovelessly had dreamed of a place where peace and tranquility prevail. A place where people live together without internal turmoil, hostility, and alienation.

Lovelessly Moreau visited the Louvre museum of art which opened in 1793 by decree of the National Assembly with a collection of five-hundred paintings including Leonardo da Vinci's masterpiece,Mona Lisa. She also views the paintings of Henry Ossawa Tanner, a black man who exiled himself from Philadelphia, Pennsylvania. With the conclusion of the American Civil War, sculptor Frederic Auguste Bartholdi decided to create a statue of liberty, to remind all Americans of the fact that black former slaves won the civil war and freed African Americans from their long night of bondage. The sculptor utilized a black woman to model for his work. At the feet, a broken shackle symbolizes a people winning their liberty.

The north was actually losing the American Civil War. The Confederates, sensing victory, turned to the offensive. General Benjamin Butler wrote to President Lincoln. "Mr. President; The north is losing…there stands a black force waiting in the wings of history, waiting to rush on stage to save us." Lincoln replied: "We will issue an emancipation document as a fit and necessary war measure, then you will have your black help." With no law barring them entry, black captives of the south left the plantations by the tens of thousands to join the union army. Whites in Boston, New York, and Philadelphia were highly offended by the inclusion of black troops. On July 13, 1863 New York's white population erupted in four days of riots. Black troops won decisive victories in the June 15, 1864 battle of Petersburg, Virginia and the September 28, 1864 battle of New Market Heights, Virginia. Even though black troops turned the tide of victory, the hate for them came from north and south. President Lincoln in his letter dated April 15, 1865 wrote: "The emancipation policy and the use of colored troops, constitute the heaviest blow yet dealt to the rebellion."

I watched the children play at Luxembourg Gardens among an array of various plants and flowers. It's a happy scene, reminding me of days long ago in San Domingo. I just wanted to lay my hand on the Eiffel Tower, feel the cold steel, and think my hand print will forever be there. The cathedral of Notre Dame is on an island in the river Seine. A palace called the Conciergeie houses the prison where Queen Marie Antoinette was imprisoned and beheaded during the revolution. I had to visit de la Bastille, where throngs stormed the facility setting-off the revolution that extended to San Domingo. A chain of events that resulted in my being in Paris. It's an amazing place, where I can still observe ramparts of the revolution on the faces of the people I meet. In Paris, there is a community of mulattos who sought education and escape from the rigors of racism. A mulatto named Oge managed to leave for England, where he boarded a brig bound for San Domingo. Oge wasted little time in convincing the island's mulattos of their dire circumstances. His call to arms resulted in Oge's capture by French soldiers. He was subsequently broken on the wheel. Oge's tragic death excited in France a wave of sympathy from the French people.

"How was your day?" Francois asks as I entered the villa.

"I'm enjoying my new home."

"You need to find something to do," he replies.

Café Montmartre is seeking a pianist to play soft tunes of mellow music while patrons sip wine. I was greeted by the manager when I entered.

"Bonjour madame."

"Bonjour monsieur."

"Comment alley-vous?"

"Bein, merci et vous?"

I played a few bars for him. I could feel he was impressed. He wanted me to start working at once. "Oui, oui. Ca vat res bien merci," I replied.

I enjoyed playing the piano while people dine and talk over their cocktails.. The restaurant served fried chicken, collard greens, macaroni and cheese, corn bread, dumplings, strawberry cheese cake all served happily by blacks just like back home. The philosopher Hegal said of the master/slave or mistress/maid relationship is the constant striving to annihilate the consciousness of the servant. When my mind drifts, my fingers usually begin playing my favorite melody. It takes me back to days long ago when life was so innocent. Peering out at the crowd, I saw a familiar face starring back. "Andrew, is that you?"

"Yes Lovelessly…I've finally found you." I took my break and came down from the piano.

"Where did you come from? How did you find me?"

"I came from London, it's across the channel. Your father's speech before the French assembly is all over the news, so I assumed you were in Paris."

"Yes but Paris is a big city."

"I've been checking café and music venues for weeks. I told you I'd never forget you."

I rushed into his awaiting arms. He kissed me gently. Andrew waited while I completed my set for the evening, then we walked arm in arm through the streets of Montmartre enjoying the shops and street stands along the way.

"What happened on the island?" Andrew asks.

"It was horrible, a massacre, my mother and Camille were murdered by rebels while I took cover in the brush outside the house. My father had a concealed passage inside his study."

"What about all those English families that escaped, then were lured back only to be killed by the rebels?"

"I don't know about that. My father and I fled to La Cap where we boarded a brig bound for France."

"Well thank God you were able to get out. The sound of your piano rings in my ear."

"Where are you staying?"

"I have a flat on Saint-Germain."

"It's really good to see you again Andrew, but I have to get home, my papa will be expecting me."

"Can I see you tomorrow?" he asks.

"Sure give me your number, I'll contact you."

Entering the villa, Lovelessly finds her father at work inside his office.

"Papa guess who I saw today?"

"That's an impossible question honey, Paris is beaucoup."

"Andrew Wells, the guy I met in San Domingo."

"The Englishman!"

"Yes!"

"I didn't like that guy from the first moment, the way he intruded when we were talking following the reception."

"I understand, yet he treated me like a gentleman should."

"The English are very deceptive…he just walked into the café in Montmartre?"

"Yes he said he had been looking for me. He has a flat on Saint-Germain."

"Just be careful! You are a woman of color. The lot of the fallen woman is tragic and lonely. A woman fallen to sexual temptation loses her virginity and her integrity. Shame is the barrier that dooms the fallen woman. When a woman is perceived as impure, she is reduced to less than, not equal to others. Remember what happened to the white women who prostituted themselves to negros in San Domingo. They were returned to France and hanged. Premarital sexual acts are a fate worse than death for women," Francois explains.

"What about the man father?"

"A man claims an element of power by reducing sexualized women to objects of pity."

While their conversation ensued, Lovelessly took note of a brief case on the desk filled with currency."

"Papa why do you have all of that money?"

"It belongs to Haiti President Jean-Pierre-Boyer, he has to appear to have clean hands."

"What does that mean? Is he paying you for the plantation?"

"I exchange his money for English pounds, German marks, Austrian shillings, or even French francs. Wherever I can obtain the highest exchange rate. We take our percentage, then it goes back to Haiti."

"I'm not sure I understand, but he must have a lot of trust in you."

"Trust is everything in a business relationship. Oh by the way, I'm thinking about a new plantation. Would you like to return to a tropical climate?"

"The islands? Does that mean slaves?"

"It's not the islands, yet slaves are key to great wealth. This will be a new adventure for both of us."

"But Papa, I'm just beginning to love Paris and French culture."

"It's just an idea, something to think about."

Lovelessly does not relish her father's idea of another plantation, yet his advise regarding libidinous conduct has sunk deep within. Entering adult life, she must plan a future of her own. She wishes for peace and happiness in the city of light.

CHAPTER 5

PARIS TO VIENNA

LOVELESSLY JOINED A WOMEN'S GROUP THAT IS PART OF A NEIGH-borhood church. During their weekly meetings, the women discuss issues regarding aspects of French society that affects their lives. Lovelessly sought opinions pertaining to sexuality that her father had talked about, and premarital sex in general. The majority seem to agree that an unmarried woman with a child is considered an outcast, a fate worse than death.

Andrew Wells and Lovelessly enjoy their time together. Whether dinning at a café in the Latin Quarter, or shopping along avenue des Champs-Elysees. Andrew takes her by train to Marseilles, in the south of France. The picturesque waterfront slums on the Mediterranean is known as the least French place in France. West Indians, north Africans, and west Africans enjoy food, wine, and song. A black man who claims he fled from America remarks that he wore glasses for years. Following six months in Paris and Marseilles he did not need the glasses at all. "All that tension had affected my sight. Suddenly as I moved through boyhood, my life switched onto the wrong track, headed down the slippery-slop of collusion and disaster. The longest lasting, most congenial and true relationship I ever enjoyed in America, was with my dog. How any self-respecting black person can live under those conditions is beyond me," he explained. Walking along the beach front, Andrew points across the Mediterranean remarking that Algeria is a country in north Africa. "France transformed Algeria from an occupied state to a colonial regime through a system of total colonization. The French military waged total war against the civilian population while the rule of law and property rights applied in occupied cities. Three-million were killed. Algerians are considered abnormal, born liars, thieves, and criminals," Andrew explains.

"It sounds like San Domingo you are talking about. I thought the world ended at the horizon, as I looked-out over the sea on the island," Lovelessly replies.

"That's exactly what I want you to understand. These measures were set into place by French Foreign Minister Alexis de Torqueville. This official traveled to America where touring the prisons, he observed millions of former slaves incarcerated. During the two-hundred forty-four year period of legal slavery, blacks were not imprisoned because their loss to the master was considered too great. Yet once they were freed, an amendment to the constitution prohibited slavery, except as a punishment for crime. The foreign minister thought that was genius. He wrote his book Democracy in America upon his return to France. What occurred in San Domingo will also occur in Cuba."

At a café in Marseilles the couple enjoy a meal of mixed seafood in rich creamy sauce, buttered carrots, and potatoes. They drink a light white wine from a fine collection. Before returning to Paris,

Andrew and Lovelessly pose for a portrait utilizing the sea as the backdrop.

"My Papa is thinking about another plantation in a tropical climate," Lovelessly explains.

"That does not surprise me, there is no limit on expansion," Andrew replies.

"Andrew do you know what it feels like to be a child of a slave?"

"No I don't, but I can tell you that slavery is the very essence of capitalism."

"My father has large amounts of money, yet he's always changing money with other countries."

While the women gather for their weekly meeting, a new member, Aurelia Davis is introduced. Aurelia Davis is recently arrived in Paris from America. She tells the group she had served in the war against England in 1812 and she merely sought peace and psychological relief in France. Lovelessly is immediately drawn to Aurelia stating similar circumstances had resulted in her arrival in Paris.

"Are you a negro?" Aurelia asks.

"I'm a French woman… did you actually fight in the war?"

"I worked for a general in Washington whose troops killed thousands of British soldiers. Following the war, he moved to Beaumont, Texas where he was assassinated by a British agent," Aurelia explains.

"I understand, so what did you do?"

"I did special assignments for the general."

"Were you a spy?"

"The British are very vindictive. They seek out those presumed enemies long after hostilities have ceased. We believed in the superiority of the white race. The British waged war for Indians and Negros."

"In San Domingo, or Haiti, the slaves completely overran the island killing all of the whites. My father, who is French, and I escaped."

"In America the ex-slaves won the civil war, but they were rewarded by being thrown into jails."

Andrew Wells' insistent pressure for sex is rejected, even-though he claims he is incapable of producing offspring for medical reasons. That made little difference, Lovelessly's father had spoken forthrightly, and his words were etched deep in her heart and mind. Lovelessly is impressed with Andrew's flat on Saint-Germin in the 7th arrondissement. The neatly arranged furnishings and carpets including a Grand piano are indicative of a man of class.

"I didn't know you played," Lovelessly says.

"Not well…my mother played, she always made the piano a fixture in our home in Kensington, the neighborhood in London where I grew-up."

"What is it that you do for a living in Paris?"

"I'm working for the government, to establish better diplomatic relations between our two countries."

"Oh so you must be going to the National Assembly building on a regular basis."

"Yes we have our office there. The National Assembly came under suspicion following the decree of May 15, 1791. It condemned slavery in principle, and remarked that the evil institution involved persons that are ignorant aliens. The whites of Port au Prince threatened secession if the mother country attempted to enforce their decree. Do you think that we will take law from the grandson of one of our slaves? They asked. No!, rather die. If France sends troops to enforce the decree, it is likely we will abandon France," Andrew explains.

"You didn't tell me that when we reconnected. I didn't know you were a government official."

"I'm on assignment in Vienna. I have to go there. Would you like to go with me.?"

"Great! I think I'd like that," she replies.

The travel by rail car consumes more than ten hours from Paris to Vienna. Lovelessly and Andrew are exhausted when they check into a hotel at Schottentor near the Ringstrasse. A bath and a good night of sleep awakens them before having breakfast at the hotel café.

"It was really difficult sleeping next to you," Andrew says.

"We can be married while we're here, then we can go for it," she says.

"I'll have to take that into consideration," he replies with a smile.

Andrew walks into the British Consulate on the Graben, talking with an official while Lovelessly looks on. Subsequently they enter stores and shops along the outdoor mall shopping before arriving at Saint Stephens Cathedral. Lovelessly is overwhelmed by the architecture and the vastness inside the sanctuary. The canal boat offers them a view of the city from the waterway flowing off the Danube river after boarding at Schwedenplatz. On the tour boat, lunch is served while they sip wine. Lovelessly notices that all the stores and shops close for business during the mid afternoon. "It's regulated, they have a socialist economic system," Andrew explains.

"That's very different than what we have in Paris," Lovelessly replies.

"Yes, I'll say, oh by the way, has your father mentioned where he plans the new plantation?"

"No…I want nothing to do with that."

They take the u-bahn to Schonbrunn Palace, tour the spacious grounds including the café before returning to the amusements at the Prader. Dinner at Café Mozart concludes the evening with grilled fish, buttered green beans, zucchini, and fried potatoes garnished with parsley. Before returning to the rail station, Andrew wants to visit Shakespeare & company booksellers on Stern gasse.

"You enjoy reading?" Lovelessly asks.

"Books rule the world…once a nation begins to think, it is impossible to stop it, says Voltaire."

"I read Shakespear's Hamlet after you quoted from King Lear," Lovelessly replies. "What a piece of work is man, how noble in faculty, how infinite in vision, in form, and moving how expressive and admirable."

"Wow! It looks like I've finally found the right girl."

"Vienna is a place that apprehends the soul, there is no revolution in the hearts of her people," Lovelessly says.

"I take it you could live here," Andrew replies.

"What is that economic system you spoke of?" Lovelessly asks.

"Under socialism the country's government centralizes all of its wealth and land for the purpose of fairly redistributing it to each member of society. Socialism lights the flame of humanity inside the hearts and minds of human beings. The state itself can diminish completely and usher in an egalitarian society. Human beings are capable of sharing the fruits of the planet equally. Under capitalism an unjust and inhuman social scheme manifests promoting private ownership of property, accumulation of wealth, profit-driven production, and the exploitation of human beings. People are in competition with one-another. Therefore a ruthless man, or a small group of such individuals grab all the land, waterways, crops, and oil deposits. The evil of capitalism is so ingrained that the very essence and quality of human life becomes contingent on personal wealth. Wealth alone becomes the measure of human worth. In a capitalist society, it is inevitable that a few men, the most ruthless, end-up controlling life itself, while the mass battle with each other for jobs that offer wages for their contribution to the development process. The social ills of racism and discrimination develop and thrive. Capitalism's dog-eat-dog philosophy inflicts dishonesty and distrust among human beings," Andrew explains.

"My head is spinning trying to keep-up with you. When you talked about controlling life itself, it made me think about slavery and my father," Lovelessly says.

Following a cup of espresso, Lovelessly falls asleep on Andrew's shoulder while the train rambles along the rails from Vienna to Paris.

CHAPTER 6

REVENGE FACTOR

AURELIA DAVIS ALWAYS TAKES PART IN DISCUSSION, SPEAKING AT the weekly meeting of the woman's group. She states that conditions for black women in the United States are far more deplorable than they had been during slavery. "Most black women are compelled to become domestic servants. They are cooks, nursemaids, and chambermaids. White women reject this line of work, while blacks hire themselves out readily. It's just as bad, if not worse than it was during slavery," Aurelia explains.

"We are informed that black women who fled the southern states for the north have a much better life," another woman replies.

"Every morning, rain or shine, groups of women stand on street corners in the Bronx and in Brooklyn waiting for a chance to get some work. Once hired, a day of back-breaking toil results in many receiving less than what they had been promised. They are forced to except used clothing rather than cash, and are exploited beyond human endurance. Only the need for money makes them submit to this daily routine," Aurelia continues.

"There was a story in the news recently, about a woman from Senegal who worked as a nursemaid for a French family in Africa. When the family returned to Paris, they asked the woman to accompany them. Once the nursemaid realized she was a mere servant, having lost contact with her family in Africa and without means to return home, she took her own life," Lovelessly explains.

Following the meeting, Aurelia approaches Lovelessly. "You are quite different than the others, where did you attend school?"

"My father had a tutor instruct me in San Domingo who taught language, music, and the arts," Lovelessly replies.

"I knew it, you listen intently…what do you do here in Paris?"

"I play the piano at Café Montmartre. Would you like to have dinner with my father and myself?"

"Yes I would like that very much," Aurelia says.

The manager at the café informs Lovelessly that her wages will be increased. Business had taken an upward turn since Lovelessly began appearing at the café, playing her renditions on the piano. Lovelessly viewed the increase as a contribution to the development process Andrew Wells had explained.

Francois Moreau received an urgent message from Haitian President Boyer. Rebels in Haiti were threatening to assassinate the president and his family. The rebels had grown tired of the murderous dictator who had stripped the nation's treasury of millions of dollars. The president sought asylum in France. Francois contacted a high official in the French government, requesting the Haitian president be given consideration. Jean-Pierre-Boyer's request is subsequently granted. A villa on the edge of Paris, surrounded by a large contingent of police, is assigned to survey the property on a round-the-clock basis.

Aurelia Davis is warmly received when she arrives at Lovelessly's home. After meeting Francois, he ushers them into the dinning area where servants prepare food and drink from a smorgasbord of hot meals including fresh salad.

"I understand you are just arrived in Paris from the United States," Francois says.

"Yes I'm still trying to decide whether or not I enjoy living in exile."

"We're all living in exile...Lovelessly tells me you worked for a general during the war."

"That's correct, general Bradley's entourage. He was assassinated by a British agent after he retired to live in Texas. I had been through the war of 1812 with him, then the American civil war. The mental toll was too much. I'm just trying to get my life together," Aurelia explains.

"Were you and the general lovers?" Lovelessly asks.

"Why else would I be with a man for that many years? We needed support from one-another."

"The fallen woman suffers a tragic and lonely existence," Francois says.

"I'm alone, but not lonely," Aurelia replies.

"During the meeting, you said black women in the U.S. were better-off during slavery."

"Yes, they are having babies at an alarming rate. The birth rate alone will eventually force whites to flee the country. Morons, mental defectives, illiterates, paupers, unemployables, criminals, and dope fiends will overtake society."

"What about white women?" Francois asks.

"White women enjoying prosperous economic conditions are urged to reproduce themselves."

"A woman cannot prevent pregnancy when she has sex," Lovelessly says.

"Black women have been aborting themselves since the earliest days of slavery. Many slave women refused to bring children into a world of forced labor where beatings and rape were everyday conditions of life. Freeing them opened the door to the booming birth rate I just spoke about," Aurelia replies.

"Eugenics is the method toward population control," Francois says.

"What is eugenics papa?" Lovelessly asks.

"It's method of improving the human species by mating those of noble birth. This would prevent morons from reproducing them-selves," Francois replies.

"With fourteen million freed negro slaves invading the north, whites are forced to turn to the south for the nation's salvation. The south is compelled to look toward white women as the medium through which we retain the supremacy of the white race over the African," Aurelia explains.

Moving into the living-room area of the house, Aurelia and Lovelessly continue their conversation while Francois returns to his office.

"Just before leaving the U.S. I received information that Francois Moreau had given Haitian rebel leaders including president for life Boyer, the idea of massacre of British subjects who had fled to America," Aurelia explains.

"I don't know anything about that...where did you get this information? Regardless, he's my father, whom I love in-spite of his sins," Lovelessly replies.

An appearance of shocked silence and disbelief on Aurelia Davis' face causes great concern from Lovelessly, as Aurelia peers at the portrait of Andrew Wells and Lovelessly at Marselles. "You obviously know this man," Aurelia says.

"Oui that's my beau," Lovelessly nervously replies.

Aurelia sits quietly for the moment, contemplating her response.

"That's the guy who killed General Bradley in Beaumont, Texas. He's a British agent, Special Branch," Aurelia says.

Lovelessly's mind flashes back to her meeting Andrew at San Domingo. He had just sailed from the U.S. southern coast. His interest in Francois' future plans. Their trip to Vienna, Austria and the talk with the official at the British Consulate. It all seemed so innocent . Suddenly Lovelessly's shoulders droop as she submerges to a state of despair.

"I should not have told you, but I had to for your own protection," Aurelia says.

"Why would Andrew kill the general?"

"It was a war…the general's troops had killed thousands of British soldiers. In war, people kill one-another, even the babies, then it's revenge, revenge, revenge that they seek. I told you that Francois may have been implicated in the massacre of British nationals who had escaped to the U.S. then were lured back to San Domingo. They were all slaughtered when they returned. Your father may be in grave danger."

"Aurelia please excuse me, but I must see Andrew."

"I understand, yet you must be very careful. If you need me, please call."

The loud knock at the door of Andrew's apartment, along with the shouting of his name, rouses the neighbors and causes the prostitute he has engaged to scramble for her things. When the door is finally opened, the lady of leisure runs past Lovelessly into the corridor and down the stairs. Andrew Wells is at a lost for words.

"Tell me why Andrew, keep it real! Why don't you love me? Is it the way I wear my hair? What can I do to be perfect for you? Why? Lovelessly pleads. "I just want the truth, even if it hurts. I need to feel loved,' she continues.

"I do love you, I'm sorry."

"You know my situation…I have no one, only my father."

"It's not you, it's me. I'm an agent of the British government… Special Branch. I was in San Domingo because your father is a suspected spy. When we were in Vienna I advised my superiors that I was in love with his daughter. The plan has been set-aside."

"We were flawed from the beginning," Lovelessly replies.

"I'm sorry…"

"It's alright, I wanted the truth."

"Can we work this out?" Andrew asks.

"Why did you kill that general in Texas?"

"You know about that…we were at war, those were my orders."

Lovelessly moves to the piano, playing while singing. "Out, out brief candle, life is but a walking shadow, a poor player who struts and frets his hour upon the stage and then is heard no more."

"I've come a long way since we met. I've changed Andrew… I can no longer be with you."

Andrew suddenly realizes that in loving her, he had taught her everything he knows about the world. She is his creation. A chasm he cannot bridge. In loving him, she had listened too well, learned too well. Now she must go from his world that threatens the life of her father.

The news shocks all of Paris when Andrew Wells is arrested by the French Police Prefecture following the murders of the former Haitian president and his wife inside their compound on the edge of the city. The heavily guarded residence of the former president was penetrated while the police guarding the entrance simply fell asleep. Following an appearance in court, Andrew is ordered to be held for trial at Bagne prison in Toulon, France on the Mediterranean coast. As court officers escort Andrew Wells out of the court-house in leg-irons, belly-chains, and hand-cuffs, Aurelia Davis steps out of the crowd, raising a hand gun she fires three rounds at point blank range, killing Andrew Wells instantly.

CHAPTER 7

NEW HORIZONS

CROWDS OF PROTESTERS GATHERED AT VARIOUS POINTS IN PARIS, demanding Aurelia Davis be hanged by the neck until she is dead inside the football stadium. Her crime of murdering the Englishman in plain view of hundreds of people was the work of the devil. It had unleashed the ghost of Toussaint Louverture. Aurelia Davis is being held at the prison on the river, where Marie Antonette was held prior to being beheaded. A lawyer for Aurelia Davis argued before a judge that Andrew Wells was a spy, working for the British Special Branch. Wells had killed an American general, madam Davis' husband, on American soil during the war of 1812. The revenge factor was therefore an act of war. Andrew Wells was in France on assignment to kill Francois Moreau, a French national who fled San Domingo but not before giving the Haitian president the idea to massacre British nationals who had escaped to the U.S. Once France granted the Haitian president asylum in Paris. Wells' assignment was altered as the former president became the top priority of the Special Branch.

Lovelessly is visibly shaken by the revelations. She suggests to her father that perhaps they should leave France for awhile, since another agent may be dispatched to Paris.

"The selection of a mate is the most consequential decision you will make in your life. By approaching you, he had access to myself," Francois replies.

"He loved to read and quote Shakespeare," Lovelessly says.

I went into my father's study once he had left the house and began reading some of his papers. I was astonished by his perception of the world and particularly that of the white race. He wrote that going forth from Europe's shores, whites have planted their laws, customs, and battle flags at the uttermost ends of the earth. The north American continent and Australia have been made virtually as white as the European motherland. South America and Africa have been extensively colonized. England's empire extends to five continents, and France holds control of large areas of Africa.

Japan's foreign policy is to exclude the white man in the far east. Japan owns the entire island chain masking the eastern sea front of Asia. Japan's population is a major problem. The country seeks lands where Japanese can breed by the tens of millions. This is the secret of her aggressive stance, her chronic imperialism, and the dream of world domination.

The English think they will rule India for centuries, taxing all of the Indian people. Where there is no white policeman, no white postman, no white colony, the empire will fall flat on its face as we did in San Domingo. Africa is a land of enormous potential wealth. The natural source of Europe's raw materials and food supply.

Missionaries must be dispatched in mass. The fierce warlike spirit inherent in Islam is more attractive than the gentle peace loving high moral standard of Christianity to the African mind. Insofar as he is Christianized, the African savage instinct is restrained and he will be disposed to white tutelage. Insofar as he is Islamized, the African's warlike posture will be unhinged, and he will seek to drive us out of Africa.

Asia may be an alternative. Vast areas of unexplored wealth, sparsely inhabited by stagnant populations. Asia like Africa must be partitioned, each section at the disposal of European nations. The man who starts with nothing, does not as a rule arrive at a livable income until he is past the marrying age. A healthy man without money is halfway sick. In Schopenhauer, one can observe the influence of Johann Wolfgang Von Goethe. To allow the tropic belt around the world to fall into Asia's hands would practically spell white race suicide.

After reading my father's papers, I agreed with him one-hundred percent. It's exactly what Andrew explained. He mentioned our disaster in San Domingo. It appears we'll be on the move. I love my father despite his sins, he's all I have. I'll just wait to see what he comes up with.

CHAPTER 8

INDOCHINA

FRANCOIS MOREAU WATCHED THE DEVELOPMENTS IN FRENCH Indochina with great interest. The missionaries were welcomed, converting a mostly Buddhist indigenous populace, to the Catholic faith in civilizing backward, uncivilized and impoverished people. In August 1858 Napoleon III attacked Da Nang, converting the area into a French military base. Two weeks later, Saigon fell to French imperialism. By 1880 Vietnam, Laos, and Cambodia are all under French control. Indochina had become the nation's most important colonial possession. Francois saw the production, profit, and labor as a means of increasing his wealth. The society itself had split along ideological and religious lines, while the introduction of troops prohibited the people from using the word "Vietnam." It is therefore called French Indochina.

Meeting with members of the Paris oligarchy at his home, Francois explains the advantages of investing in Indochina. "Vietnam stands at the hub of a vast area of the world. He who holds or has influence can affect the future of all of southeast Asia's two-hundred forty-nine million people. Huge rice surpluses, rubber, tin, and oil are ours for the taking. Vietnam is a gold mine, waiting to be explored and exploited," he explains.

"How can we expect to control this vast population you speak of, this can be another San Domingo," one of the men replies.

"This time we will not transport millions of black Africans from across the sea, we learned our lesson. We can exploit the local populace. They live in small villages and are seldom affected by outside events. They know little of what is going-on beyond the huts and fields they till for crops, and the streams they fish in their sampans," Francois explains.

"The rice crop and rubber will result in handsome return. We can market rice in Saigon and across the country, however it will be difficult to control fishing," another investor says.

"What about the labor you spoke about?"

"Coolies will work for a few piastres, which are nothing to the franc. One franc is worth more than one-hundred piastres. Eventually when they adopt the language and culture, we will own the labor," Francois says.

"Are you speaking of human trafficking?"

"Yes of course, we will have complete control."

The French East India company had set-up operations in 1668, establishing a pattern which continued for centuries. The government raised money by selling securities to the East India company which effectively became an important owner of the national debt.

When Lovelessly and her father arrive in Saigon, 5,000 Frenchmen rule over a country of 30,000,000 Vietnamese. Francois completed the purchase of a plantation north of Saigon. The 15,000 acres of rubber trees is one of the largest in the country. Awaking in the morning, the smell of rubber has replaced the sounds of Paris for Lovelessly. The weather is hot, temperatures reach above one-hundred degrees daily year-round. Humidity brings the monsoon season. The army of coolies Francois hires are poverty stricken and desperate for income. He pays them at the rate of 57 piastres a day, or half of one franc for draining the sap from the trees. A Chinese Mandarin serves as supervisor,.from dawn to dusk. The overseer pressures this army of labor exposed to the burning sun, spurred on by the whip and eye. Once the coolies become attached to the plantation, Francois changes the method of payment by giving his workers rice, which they eat daily. The rice is obtained from farmers and on the black market.

A lucrative contract with French multi-national Michelin tire provides a handsome outlet for his product. When French nationals are attacked, injured, or killed, the military merely utilizes these incidents to extend authority.

Lovelessly views Saigon as the Paris of the orient. Wide palm tree lined boulevards and stylish French restaurants, exhibit the best of France. The Ben Nghe canal flows into southwest Saigon, offset by the pineapple orchids. She loves the outdoor café and modern buildings that resemble Paris. The breathtaking view of hills and mountains rising out of lakes and streams with low-lying clouds surrounding the peaks makes for a spectacular show of nature. Francois encouraged Lovelessly to teach the Vietnamese children the language at the school in Cholon. "Language is everything, the

Vietnamese have adopted it and French culture. It commands the heart and mind," he says. The school also educated Vietnamese in French history, literature, math, science, and law. Lovelessly enjoys the environment and the children. The older women are called "mama san", while older men are referred to as "papa san", from Japanese dialect. The people have combined the Vietnamese, Japanese, and French languages. Lovelessly is proud of the way she helps bring civilization to Indochina, yet there are many who wish to rid their country of French rule. As a consequence, armed resistance will continue throughout the entire period.

CHAPTER 9

LAW OF THE LAND

A BREAK IN THE SCHOOL YEAR SET ME BACK TO MY NORMAL ROU-
tine of awakening each morning to the smell of rubber. The coolies work from well before dawn until late in the evening, usually
fifteen hours or more. It's a dreary existence, reminiscent of my
childhood days. With the developed mind and eye, I feel the effect
of Andrew's words. Life on a rubber plantation is dull and boring
because it's always dark, with diminished light. The thick heavy
foliage of the rubber trees completely blot-out the rays of the sun.
These strange little men wearing their head gear with the light fixture allows them to focus on the tree trunk while draining the sap
into buckets. Carlee once told me that the slaves in San Domingo
constantly thought of attacking the overseer and killing the master.
Yet their only escape was the sea, and they had no access to ships.
It's very different in Indochina. The Mandarin who beats coolies
for not working fast enough, places himself in a precarious position. These coolies are at home. This is their land, they are familiar
with all of the surrounding countryside. The many wide tracts of
tangled mountains, covered with impenetrable tropical forests are
inaccessible. To limit or minimize this threat, Mandarins, whole

communities, and religious groups are set against one another. The country itself is divided into three large provinces, with a corrupt administrator selected by the French government. It's divide and rule. The use of the word Vietnam is declared illegal.

In San Domingo, our island was divided in-half. The west is now Haiti, while the east is Dominican Republic. Profit is the main objective of our presence in Indochina. Colonial officials and French multi-national companies have taken control of the land and made it into large plantations, increased production, exports, and paid slave wages or no wages at all. Rice, rubber, and sugar are the main cash crops. The amount of land used for growing rice has quadrupled in the past year. Indochina is supplying 60,000 tons of rubber each year, while we have built factories and the railroad to extract coal, tin, and zinc. Most of the material is sold abroad as exports, while the profits line the pockets of French capitalists like my father. He has so much money it's unbelievable. What is he going to do with all of it? He can't spend that money. I keep hearing the voice of Andrew Wells. The relationship between big money and war is so close, that their economic activity is a direct cause for war. The money class constantly seeks new markets to invest their surplus. As a consequence, increasing capital does not find investment in full, in a country where the free market system is already in-place. Therefore the money class seeks to invest part of their surpluses in a country like Indochina, where free market capitalism has not penetrated, and is under threat of repressive communism. If the inhabitants of Indochina are opposed to this, the resulting antagonism usually leads to war. Some of the whites are former confederate soldiers who fled the United States following defeat in the civil war. They merely seek fortune, while attempting to initiate racism with their flag of slavery. There are students at the school in Cholon the people call "nguoi phan quec," traitor. They often hold high positions, even "banque de indochine," the French bank of Indochina. Some are given scholarships to study in France, and a few are granted French citizenship. I'm teaching children to speak French, while the overall philosophy is the supremacy of French values and culture. My only real peace comes when I relax at the piano, delving deep into my music. I feel exploited in my own world.

The railroad system was completed to connect people in various parts of the country according to the government. They call it the unification of Indochina. In reality, it exports agriculture products, mail sent to Paris, and whatever else that needs to be transported. I boarded the train at Saigon, intent on making the 1,100 mile journey to Hanoi. The train made station stops in Bien Hoa, Dalat, Cam Ranh, Nha Trang, Tuy Hoa, Da Nang, Hue, and Hanoi. The breathtaking view produced by nature in the countryside is something I can never forget. In Phan Rang province, herds of elephant played with their young, large birds hovered overhead, while oxen grazed in the grass. There are plantations everywhere. Rubber, sugarcane, and rice patties consume the plains. We traveled through three or four tunnels in Dalat. Here is a place in the central highlands, built by the French. Large single villas with swimming pools and tennis courts, offset by tall palm trees. A large lake in the center of town is a place of leisure where people paddle around the waters in small boats. The higher altitude means the temperature is not as high. This is the life of the bourgeoisie.

Nha Trang is another resort city on the South China sea, similar yet smaller than Saigon. After crossing the Red River bridge at Long Bien, we stopped for about one hour. I utilized the time to walk into a small village. A single unpaved strip, lined by shanty's on either side is home to hundreds of Vietnamese. Children rushed toward me, looking for anything I could give them. I felt ashamed and embarrassed by their ragged clothing and bare feet. A candle flickered in the window of a hut. A child's eyes reflect dreams sealed in the heart. A French soldier tosses a few candies onto the ground. He seems amused watching the children scramble for the pieces. The children are every race and color in the universe. They are the ultimate victims. There is much soul debt in this place. The candle still flickers in the window of the hut as I return to the train. The children's dreams are sealed in the heart.

Many of the causes of the French revolution are present in Indochina. Miserable housing, poverty, lack of freedom and equality. How can the French people come into a country, build-up a place like Dalat for themselves, then expect to live in peace while protected by their soldiers? It's San Domingo…different sides of the same coin. My father and his friends are the direct cause for war. We have come to Indochina, where capitalism has not penetrated, and we can excuse ourselves by claiming it is under pressure of communism. Hanoi is a city much like Saigon. There are places so similar to Paris, they would be difficult to distinguish in a photo. I checked into the Continental Hotel, took a nice bath, then had a meal at the dinning-room. While waiting to be served, a man approached asking whether he could join me at the table? He introduced himself as Jules Martin.

"I saw you walk in, are you French?" he asked.

"Yes French and African. I am Lovelessly Moreau from Saigon."

"I am French and Vietnamese, nice to meet you Lovelessly. What brings you to Hanoi?"

"I haven't been in Indochina very long and I wanted to see the country."

"Ah… so you are from Paris."

"How did you know that?"

"I can hear the accent."

I began to relax for some strange reason with that remark. "Do you live in Hanoi?"

"No, just north of here, I'm a student at the university."

"It appears the whole country is plantations."

"The French have taken all of the land, they claim it as their own. They make laws, giving the land to these people who call it private property. The children cannot go there anymore, they cannot play anywhere. What are the children to do? Boys will be criminals, girls will be prostitutes. It's the law of the land, made by the almighty white man. The concept of white supremacy is therefore instilled under the guise of law by the colonizer."

"Just like San Domingo, the island where I was born"

"I thought you said Paris."

"We moved to Paris after San Domingo was overrun by rebels."

"I've studied San Domingo. We admire the courage of the black slaves and their fight for freedom in Haiti. We have community meetings, where each person talks about their personal problems. We discovered that all of our problems come from French pressure in Vietnam. Asian people love stage plays, where characters play-out our problems through the actors. They always conclude: Death to land robbers! Death to mandarins!"

"In San Domingo people were divided into three racial classes, 28,000 whites 22,000 mulattos, and 405,000 negro slaves. The idea was to turn the mulattos against the blacks, but that failed because a black leader, Toussaint Louveture trained an army to overthrow the French."

"A leader always arises from an oppressed people. You said we moved to Paris! Do you have a husband?"

"No it's just my father and I."

"Is he a land owner?"

"Yes he owns a rubber plantation near Saigon."

"Are the coolies slaves?"

"They are paid slave wages. I'm teaching the language at a school in Cholon."

"I understand why you are searching, it's a bad situation for you Lovelessly."

"My papa is my only family., My mama and step-mom were killed by rebels in San Domingo."

"Plantation owners in America blamed abolitionists for slave revolts. Plantation owners in Vietnam blame communists for slave revolts. The basic factor in human affairs is not politics but race."

"That's exactly what my father says," Lovelessly replies.

"The opium trade makes more money on the black market than rubber, rice, sugar, and tin combined."

"Who is trading opium?"

"Corrupt officials the French have placed in charge. They bring chemists from Thailand and Burma to cultivate the opium into #4 grade heroin, which is 80 to 90% pure. You said you teach in Cholon! Cholon is known for its opium dens. Asian bagpipes play music, while lighted multi-colored figurines revolve casting eerie images onto the walls, while people smoke and pass the pipes containing the drug. They use the Ben Nghe canal to move the drug into the delta for shipment to Marseille. I cannot count the number of corpses dragged from the canal. Ho Chi Minh opposed the opium trade. He said the French were pushing opium on the people of Vietnam as a means of social control. Drugged people are less likely to rise-up and throw off the oppressor. Ho Chi Minh had been asking American presidents since Lincoln for help in ridding the nation of the French."

"How do you know about this?"

"My father…he was a French naval officer. He spoke-out against what the government is doing. He called this a dirty war. French officers are forbidden to show public affection for a Vietnamese woman, yet he did. As punishment, they sent him to

Dragon Island, in the Bay of Ha Long. Coolies are subjected to unspeakable torture and restrain before being sold at auction, if they are still alive."

"Human trafficking?"

"Yes chattel slavery…people are preparing for a major assault. Soon blood will flow from Hanoi to Saigon. Should you remain in Vietnam, you will risk great danger. They call us communists, Viet Minh, it makes no difference, we are Vietnamese fighting for our nation"

"Where is your father?"

"In a Paris jail…what did you do in Paris?"

"I played the piano at Café Montmartre."

Arriving back home in Saigon, Francois is filled with anxiety. "Where have you been, I've had everyone looking for you?"

"I took the train to Hanoi, I wanted to see the country."

"Hanoi! Holy shit, that's full of communists."

"The whole countryside is nothing but plantations, just like San Domingo. The people are huddled-up in small villages, shanty's and huts."

"You didn't need to see any of that, there is nothing to be gained."

"Papa I'm going back to Paris."

"What on earth for… there's money to be had here."

"They are planning an assault, it's going to be worse than the island. Papa, you made slaves of Africans in San Domingo, you want Vietnamese to be your slaves. Can't you see that in both cases there is nothing but war and the blood of innocents? It just doesn't work the way you think it should."

"We don't have to worry about that, the government has plenty of troops to protect us."

"Papa you are too old and self-centered, we need to leave, remember what happened to my mom and step-mom back on the island."

"How dare you talk to me like that, you of diminished linage. I named you after I married Camille without love, whom God had withheld the fruit of the womb. I was angry because I wanted a child very much. Camille urged me to lay with Carlee, her servant, an African woman. Now you have come against me. I set this whole thing up, I have a shipment coming soon from Thailand."

"A shipment from Thailand…what are you talking about?"

"Opium! I'm making more money on this stuff than I'll ever get from those stupid rubber trees. They buy it like crazy, they can't get enough. Our soldiers run a much greater risk of becoming heroin addicts than a combat casualty. The troops spend eighty million a year on heroin from the Golden Triangle to Da Nang, where it is picked-up and sent to Saigon."

"Papa you are off the rails, I'm getting out of here."

Crowds gathered along Cong Ly boulevard in front of the presidential palace, waiting for a public statement regarding the rebel group called Viet Minh. The president wished to calm fears of another outbreak of violence, while presiding over huge expansions in Saigon's opium parlors in order to line his pockets. Buddhist monks in accord with their religious teaching set themselves aflame in mass suicide in the streets. The Buddhist cardinal vices of lust, sloth, avarice, and pride are voiced as the cause. Envy and hatred is also included The government in Paris dispatched two ocean-liners into the gulf south of Saigon with orders to transport French citizens desirous of leaving Indochina.

The Viet Minh assault is coordinated to begin simultaneously at Hue, Chi Lai, Bien Hoa, Nha Trang, and Long Binh. Eventhough Lovelessly pleads with her father, Francois is set in his ways and is unwilling to flee.

"The Viet Minh are seeking to take back Indochina. Through the veil of pretence, hypocrisy, lies and deception, the world of soldiers, doctors, lawyers, and priests wear masks that conceal money-grubbers. Man is at bottom a dreadful wild animal, cultured to exist in what we call civilization.

We are shocked therefore by outbreaks like the revolution in France. When the bolts and bars of the legal order fall apart, it reveals society for what it is. The reply received by the British anti-slavery society from the American anti-slavery society in response to the treatment of slaves in America illustrates the horror visited upon those unhappy people. The human harshness and cruelty reveals how these devils in human form, these bigoted, church-going scoundrels treat these innocent black people. Little wonder the British government responded by waging the war that sent Andrew to America," Lovelessly explains.

"This Brit Andrew, has really done a job on your psychological disposition. The British themselves are devils. In the year 1848 it is revealed that hundreds of couples poisoned their children, one after another, or tortured them to death with hunger and neglect merely for the insurance money," Francois replies.

"There is a famous water-color painting by Tischbein which depicts a son bearing his aged father on his back while fleeing the stream of lava rushing down the mountain-side towards the sea. When only a narrow strip of land between the two destructive elements remains, the father tells the son to lay him aside and save himself, lest they both should perish. The son obeys, yet looks back for one last look at his father. The Viet Minh are the lava between us and the sea," Lovelessly says

"Daughter I have too much invested. This republic will one day be hailed as the greatest conquest of the French empire. I cannot turn my back on the opportunity to be part of that."

"Republics are anti-natural, artificial and derive from reflection. There are very few of them in the history of mankind. The Greek and Roman empires come to mind. They were made possible by the fact that 5/6 or 7/8 of their populations were slaves. The case is similar in the United States. In 1840 a population of sixteen-million consists of three-million slaves, and they are counted as 3/5 of a person according to their constitution. Republics are easy to establish, yet hard to maintain. Precisely the opposite is true of monarchies," Lovelessly replies.

Human blood poured forth in torrents, the earth blackened with the ash of mortar shells. The air is tainted with pestilence. Thousands of French nationals are massacred, homes and buildings on the plantations are consumed in flame. Thousands of Viet Minh are killed, yet they fight on in their push towards Saigon. The hatred for the French runs so deep, ears are cut-off dead soldiers, while testicles are severed and jammed into the mouths of dead combatants. The Viet Minh are monsters of cruelty. The scattered white population of the plantations can offer little resistance to the well armed Viet Minh rebels. The men are killed at once, their women and children unfortunate victims. The entire horizon is a wall of fire from which thick black smoke rolls onward, blocking-out the sun's rays. Viet Minh troops never cease to burn anything to feed the flames. Plains are covered by the smoldering ash as far as the eye can see. A sight more terrible than the mind can comprehend. Among the prisoners taken by French troops, are several whites. They are willing to see Saigon go down in blood and fire, as long as they share in the plunder. Black troops are former slaves who believe their service in forcing slavery upon another people of color is actually of redeeming value. An embargo is placed on all vessels, to serve as refuse, yet overloading causes a brig to capsize in the bay resulting in the drowning of hundreds. The Vietnamese army turns pacifist, resorting to looting and stealing in the plunder and flame of Saigon.

CHAPTER 10

LOVELESSLY

MY BELOVED COUNTRY WITH THE BLESSING OF THE UNITED States of America is sending 200,000 of our best young men to Indochina. This is the nation's reaction to the loss of empire. The lost implies a revision of national identity. The women in my church group welcomed me back with open arms. They also talked about the "dirty war" in Indochina. The naval officer who objected to our policy was subjected to the punishment of witnessing human auctioning and subsequent incarceration here at home.

I had been having nightmares regarding the horrors of San Domingo, and now Indochina. I think about both places every day to the point of mental exhaustion. I pray for my father. My only happiness is sleep, hopefully without the nightmares, yet when I awaken, the mental pain persists. I'm alone in Paris, the vastness of my father's house. What am I to do with myself? I must find work. Work will fill the void of my loneliness. The worker is a commodity. She is fortunate to find a buyer. Therefore her life is regulated by the will of the oligarchs. The more the worker wants to earn, the more she must sacrifice in terms of time and freedom like the slaves of San Domingo and Indochina. Ultimately our lives are shortened. When the state declines economically, misery increases among the working class. Consequently when the state advances economically there is complicated misery. Misery is always the constant of the working class. To control population, surplus will have to die. In England 1857 there are 60,000 to 70,000 prostitutes. The life span of these ladies of the streets runs six or seven years. To maintain the level of 60,000 to 70,000 prostitutes there must be 80,000 women each year who will take-up the infamous trade. Therefore the theory of labor as a commodity is nothing short of a disguised theory of slavery. Labor is life, exchanged for food. Where human life is regarded as a commodity, we are forced to admit slavery. The acquisition of new territory increases the stock, profit, and wealth of the oligarchs.

The huge profits taken by landlords increases the misery The greater the misery, the higher the rent. The wealthy live off the interest of their capital. The right of landowners and robbery are different sides of the same coin. They love to reap where they have not sowed, exploiting the natural resources. The objective is to make as much money as possible while decreasing the wage of the worker.

When two officials from the Foreign Ministry appeared at my door, I felt something was wrong. They explained, "Francois Moreau has been killed in Cholon, by Viet Minh rebels." I burst into tears. An official of the National Assembly stated "off the record," that the British Special Branch had placed an agent in Saigon who targeted Francois Moreau. "Life is like the sea, full of dips and whirlpools, which man avoids with the greatest care and solicitude, although he knows that even if he succeeds in getting through with all his efforts and skill, he yet by doing so comes nearer at every step to the greatest, the total, inevitable and unavoidable shipwreck, death," says Schopenhauer.. We crossed the sea together, from San Domingo to Paris, and from Paris to Saigon. I have lost both parents through the hate generated by exploited manipulated humans, called rebels, for wanting freedom. I also lost the only man I ever loved through war and retaliation. My father's estate is valued at millions of francs, yet I feel depression creeping forward with every passing day.

Inside Francois' office, I entered a vestibule he set-up to provide additional security. I found a cache of gold coins and bars, in addition to paper currency. Fiat money or paper is a currency that a government declares to be legal tender, even though it has no intrinsic value. Fiat money is ultimately based upon enough people having faith that a given currency will be accepted for the purpose of economic transactions. A note in my father's handwriting explains: "Paper money is obviously the invention of the devil. It is already in circulation. It is nearly worthless following the revolution in France due to the rapidly ensuing hyperinflation." I often wondered whether my father really loved me? A human being who seeks to be loved, cannot compete with their loved-one's love of money. Money is the master. The individual a mere commodity, utilized for a specific period of time. Andrew Wells taught me these lessons. In money, Andrew said, social relationships among human beings are like a thing. The analogy between human slavery and capitalism hints at the nature of capitalism itself. Money is the pimp between man's need, between his life and the means of life. All things exchange for money. Love becomes money, money becomes love.

Abraham Lincoln's greenback system followed the same path, yet the U.S. dollar is the currency of choice in the purchase of crude oil. The American Civil War disrupted the economy and compelled radical changes in the monetary system. War related expenses forced the U.S. government off the gold standard and into fiat money. With the means at my disposal, one might think I am a happy person. Nothing could be further from the truth. Money does not make of a happy person. There is alienation of nature, alienation of others, and alienation of one's self. Suicide is not something to be taken lightly, yet it remains an acceptable option for a character as in the drama of Euripides. A character faced with the foreseeable future of shame, dishonor, and unbearable suffering may seek to escape from a loveless existence or anything painful. To fly from evil or trouble is to lack courage, or that which Aristotle calls a coward. Courage involves the willingness to confront that which may result in serious negative consequences, yet one freely chooses to face the danger. The soldiers marching into Indochina face the sacrifice for the preservation of the motherland.

Escaping from life by one's own hand is likened to a disgraceful flight before the enemy. Yet I had no just cause to be in Indochina. My mother was a slave, torn from her African home. Flight from evil is just. The devil needs an instigator. An act of injustice towards one's self is the epitome of cowardice. When an individual commits murder, it is a crime against the state. It follows that an individual who kills themselves commits an act against the state. However, in cases of suicide, we witness the cause as mental health, or blame the victim. The state creates the psychological disposition of the individual.

In the solitude of my dream, I envision our soldiers meeting their defeat in Vietnam at Dien Bien Phu, just north of Hanoi. The United States will take-up the fight where we have failed. Another great American president stands in the shadow of Lincoln. He too will face the assassin's bullet. Lincoln was concerned about slavery in America, Kennedy will be concerned about the civil rights of blacks in America, and slaves in Indochina. Both these presidents are shot on Friday with strikes to the head. One is elected in 1860, the other in 1960. John Fitzgerald Kennedy explains: "It is now well known that we were at one time on the brink of war in Indochina. A war which could well have been more costly, more exhausting, and less conclusive than any war we have ever known. The threat of such war is not now altogether removed from the horizon." History is no strange place. Its relation to location is only akin to repetition of events in different configurations. My maturity is solely the work of experience, and consequently of time.

I attempted to convince my father that what he was doing in San Domingo and Indochina was wrong. Ultimately, France created the situation in Haiti by exporting more than 400,000 Africans from their homeland to the island to be their slaves. The French simply overwhelmed themselves with greed that resulted in disaster. The world's only country founded by former slaves is presided over by corrupt leaders like the former president Andrew assassinated in Paris. France will claim they are alarmed by the horrendous condition of the Haitian people, yet they will call for a global response wilfully failing to accept responsibility. The country will maintain excellent relations with the Dominican Republic, the island's eastern sector, maintaining an Embassy in Santo Domingo which monitors trade, educational and cultural exchange. French tourists will visit the country often. Haiti's future of abject poverty, corruption, and gang violence will become common-place. I recall hearing a Frenchman at San Domingo say…one of three things would happen, the whites would exterminate the entire mulatto caste, the mulattos would destroy the whites, the negro would profit from this division and annihilate both whites and mulattos. The whites of LaCap finally acknowledged the ownership of land at San Domingo belonged to the negro. Indochina on the other hand presented a vastly different set of circumstances. The Vietnamese people had lived there for centuries before Napoleon III attacked DaNang in the 1850's. I withheld from my father the fact that a network of tunnels throughout the country would result in the massacre of untold numbers of French troops.

I was inside a shop on Champs-Elysees when I felt the burning stare of a stranger. Looking-up abruptly, a tall handsome man smiled back at me. At that moment, I realized I was peering into the future and the eyes of my husband. We are strangers when we meet, yet for one to love, it is not necessary that much time should pass, that at the first and only glance a certain correspondence and consonance on both sides has occurred, which we are want to call the special influence of the stars. His name is Marcel, from Versailles. We are married in Paris. It was Shakespeare who wrote "Whoever loved who loved not at first sight?"

THE END

Printed in the United States
by Baker & Taylor Publisher Services